I Can and I Did!

Scott Dietrich Publications
Dietrich, Scott D. 1978-
I Can and I Did!
ISBN 978-0-9880534-0-3

D1530191

This book is dedicated to those who have a dream and
are committed to making it happen.
Let passion be your guide, not fear.
Face challenges head on and with a smile because
whether you think you can, or whether you
think you can't, you're right.

"I can't do this." Stephanie shouted out loud.

Stephanie's grandfather, lovingly known as "Gramps", was startled by the sudden noise. Nearly jumping out of his chair, he braced himself and said "What, what do you mean?"

"I've been trying to solve this math problem and well, I just can't." Stephanie said.

"How do you know you can't?" Gramps inquired, lowering his reading glasses into his lap.

Stephanie looked puzzled for a moment and then responded, "Because I've been trying and I just can't."

"Well, then you're right." He put his reading glasses back on and continued with his crossword.

Now Stephanie looked really confused. "What do you mean I'm right?"

"Oh I'm sorry, no one told you? Can and can't are magic words." Gramps replied.

"Huh?" Stephanie blurted out. You could tell she was confused because her head was tilted to one side just like her dog Dizzy when he's confused.

"Well, the way it works is quite simple," Gramps explained. "Whether you think you can or whether you think you can't, you're right."

"Are you sure about that Gramps?" Stephanie asked.

Gramps sat up straight in his chair, took off his reading glasses and said, "As sure as I am the sky is blue."

"Well then why haven't I heard this before?" Stephanie pressed.

Her Grandfather motioned her closer, looked around to make sure no one was listening and whispered, "Because it's a secret."

Stephanie stood straight up with hands on her hips. "Now why would people keep that a secret?"

"Shhh, shhh, shhh. Because you have great power Stephanie."

"Me?" Stephanie asked as her head tilted to one side again.

"Everyone." Gramps answered.

"Everyone?" Stephanie said shocked.

"Everyone." Gramps insisted.

"What kind of powers?" Stephanie questioned.

Pointing his finger to the sky to make his point.
"You can do, be, or have anything you believe you can."

"Now I know you're joking." Stephanie laughed.

Gramps bushy eyebrows rose. "I'm actually quite serious."

"But I've been working on this math problem all morning and I just can't do it. I really can't. Where are my powers now when I really need them?" Stephanie said.

"If you say you can't enough, and you really believe it, then you won't be able to. Your wish will come true." He explained.

"I never wished this." Stephanie insisted.

"You may as well have. You don't realize your own power do you?"

"I guess not, could you show me?" Stephanie asked.

"I thought you would never ask. Let's pretend that you could solve that math problem, it was just a matter of how. How would you say that?" Gramps questioned.

"Well, I guess I would say, I can, I just don't know how yet." Stephanie replied.

"Very good. There is magic in those words. You never doubted that you could find the answer. You believed you could even before you did it." Gramps explained proudly.

"But I still don't know the answer." Stephanie said.

"Let's work on that." Gramps said.

So they sat down and worked on the problem together. It took a few minutes but Stephanie found the answer. At which point she leapt up on her chair, threw her arms in the air and shouted, "I did it Gramps, I figured it out!"

"I am very proud of you." Gramps glowed.

"Thanks a lot Gramps."

"Oh, no thanks necessary. I knew you had it in you. Sometimes we need to ask others for help though, and that's okay. But never say can't. Can't and never are forever. And I didn't believe for one minute that you would never be able to solve that problem. Did you?" He asked.

"No, I guess not. I just got frustrated." Stephanie admitted.

"Don't worry, it happens to everybody." Gramps said.

"Even you Gramps?" Stephanie asked.

"Even me," he sighed. "If you can believe it, there was a time when I didn't believe I could fly."

"What?" Stephanie's eyes widened with amazement "You can fly?"

"Do you want to see?" he asked.

"Do I ever!" Stephanie squeaked.

So they hopped into Gramps old station wagon and drove downtown to the aviation museum. Stephanie could hardly contain her excitement. Every two minutes she would ask if they were there yet and when was she going to see him fly.

When they got there, they stopped briefly at the ticket booth. Stephanie's grandfather opened his wallet and flashed a card to the lady behind the counter. She grinned and waved them in.

"What's that card you showed the lady back there?" Stephanie inquired.

"Oh, I've got a special membership here." Gramps explained.

They continued down a long, dark hallway with flickering lights that buzzed like mosquitoes.

At the end of the hall, they entered a gigantic room called a hangar. It was the biggest room Stephanie had ever seen. It was the size of several football fields side-by-side. The room was filled with planes, loads of them. Some were very old and some very new.

It was breathtaking. Stephanie just stood there, with arms at her sides and mouth wide open. When Gramps noticed, he chuckled and asked, "What do you think?"

"Wow! These planes are so cool Gramps," Stephanie said. "I wish I could fly them."

From the corner of the room, a tall woman in a uniform started walking towards them. She waved at Stephanie's Grandfather.

"Hello Captain," she said.

"Captain? Is Gramps a pilot?" Stephanie thought to herself.

"Hello Sue." Gramps waved his hand to the woman in the uniform.

"So Captain, is this your granddaughter?" the woman asked.

She also appeared to be a pilot.

"She sure is." Gramps playfully messed Stephanie's hair with his big hand.

"Sue this is Stephanie, Stephanie this is Sue."

"Nice to meet you," Stephanie said, as she reached up and shook Sue's hand. "Are you both pilots?"

"She doesn't know?" Sue exclaimed to Gramps.

"Cat's out of the bag now," Gramps laughed. It was a saying her grandfather used whenever Stephanie figured something out.

"Your grandfather is a very important person around here. Take a look at this picture." Sue pointed to a black and white photo in a little stand beside an old plane.

It was Stephanie's grandfather sitting in the cockpit of that very plane. He was wearing a uniform that looked similar to the one Sue was wearing but he was wearing a helmet and goggles. At that moment, Gramps and Sue noticed Stephanie staring at the picture with mouth wide open. All the pieces had come together.

"Not only is your grandfather a pilot, he was my teacher," Sue exclaimed. "He taught me how to fly."

This was almost more then Stephanie could take in all at once.

She slowly looked up from the picture towards her grandfather, completely star-struck, and said, "You really can fly."

"So could you, but only if you believe you can," Gramps said as he gave her a big wink.

She gulped. "Really?"

"Well, what do you say Sue, want to join us for a spin?" Gramps asked.

"Would love to, Captain," Sue eagerly replied.

"Has Gary finished the repairs on my plane?" Gramps inquired.

"Yep, he finished yesterday," Sue confirmed. "She's ready to fly."

"Whoa, whoa, whoa. Are you saying what I think your saying? Are we going for a ride, in a plane right now?"

"Yes Stephanie," Gramps chuckled.

"Eeeeeeeeeeeeeeeee!" Stephanie squealed with delight as Gramps and Sue quickly shoved their fingers in their ears.

Sue left to go prepare the plane. Stephanie and Gramps continued to walk around the museum. Stephanie busied herself asking Gramps a million questions about being a pilot and Gramps was happy to share every last detail.

About a half hour later, they met Sue on the runway.

Stephanie's grandfather had to show his special card again to get clearance to this very private area.

Sue helped Stephanie and her grandfather onto the plane. It was a small plane that only seated four.